The Shiny Key

Titles in the series

Kipper and the Giant

Robin Hood

The Laughing Princess

The Shiny Key

Red Planet

Lost in the Jungle

The Shiny Key

Story by Roderick Hunt

Illustrations by Alex Brychta

OXFORD
UNIVERSITY PRESS

Chip was watching television.

The magic key was on the arm of the chair.

Nadim came to play.

Chip didn't want to play.

He wanted to watch television.

He wanted to watch a programme about magpies.

Nadim wanted a magic adventure.

Chip looked for the magic key, but he couldn't find it.

Nadim helped Chip to look.

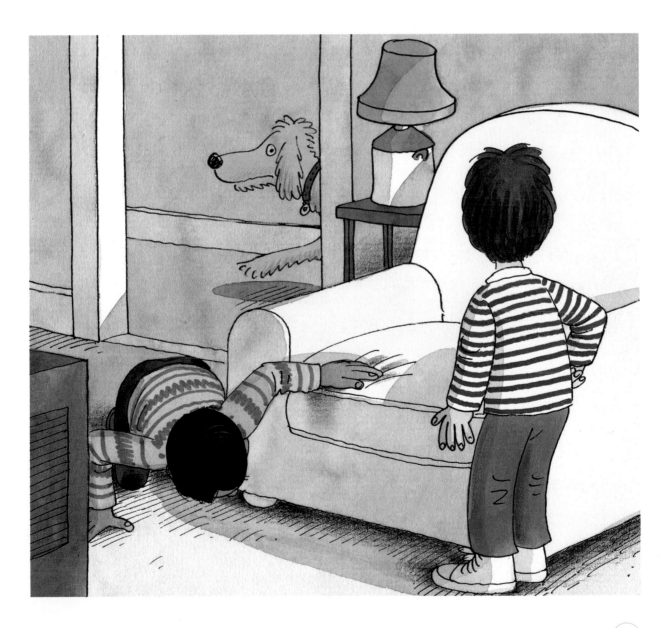

Chip looked at the armchair.

'I put the key on the arm of the chair,' he said.

Suddenly, he had an idea.

The children looked in the armchair.

They found lots of things.

Chip found Mum's missing ear-ring.

'Mum will be pleased,' he said.

Chip found the key.

It was stuck to a toffee.

'Yuk!' said Chip.

'It's all sticky.'

Chip told Mum about the armchair.

He gave Mum the missing ear-ring.

Nadim cleaned the key.

He made it very shiny.

The children went to Biff's room.

Biff looked at the key.

'Oh no! It looks very shiny,' she said.

'I hope the magic still works.'

Suddenly, the key began to glow.

It looked very bright.

The magic took the children into

a new adventure.

The children were in a wood.

Chip didn't like it.

The wood was dark and gloomy.

'Come on!' he said.

Suddenly, Biff saw something shiny.

She picked it up.

'What a beautiful ring!' she said.

'Somebody must have dropped it.'

The children saw some soldiers.

The soldiers saw the ring.

They grabbed the children.

'That ring is stolen,' they said.

The soldiers took the children to the prince.
'We've found the thieves,' they said. 'Here's
your ring.'

'Here are the thieves,' said the prince.

'What else have they stolen?'

'My watch was stolen,' said a man.

'My ear-ring was stolen,' said a lady.

A soldier took the magic key.

'Look at this shiny key,' he said.

'These children have stolen things.

They must have locked them away.'

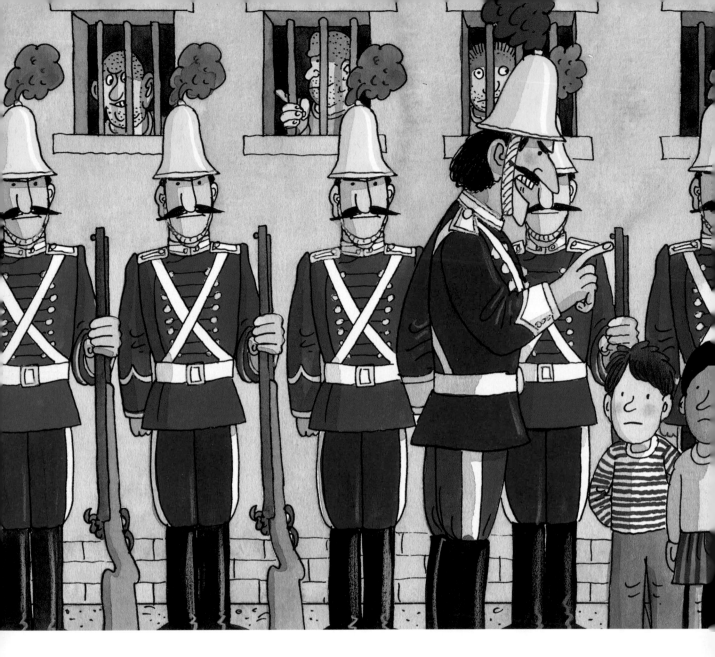

The soldiers took the children to a prison.

'Where are the stolen things?' they asked.

'Tell us, or we'll lock you up.'

Suddenly, a magpie flew down.

It took the magic key.

'Stop that magpie!' called Biff.

'It's stolen the key.'

The magpie flew to the woods.

'The magpie is the thief,' said Chip.

The children ran after the magpie.

Everyone ran after the children.

The magpie flew to a tree.

'Look in its nest,' said Chip.

Nadim climbed the tree.

'Be careful,' called Biff.

Nadim looked in the magpie's nest.

It was full of shiny things.

Nadim gasped.

'What beautiful things!' he said.

'You see!' said Anneena, crossly.

'We aren't thieves.

The magpie took your things.'

'Sorry!' said the soldier.

Everyone was pleased.

'Here's my missing ear-ring,' said a lady.

'Here's my watch,' said a man.

The prince gave the children a medal.

'The magpie was the thief,' he said.

'Sorry, we thought it was you.'

The magic key began to glow.

'Magpies like shiny things,' said Biff.
'So it was a good job Nadim made the
magic key shiny, after all.'

Questions about the story

- Where did the Magic Key get lost?
- Why did Nadim clean the key?
- Who went on this Magic Key adventure?
- How can you tell they went to a different country?
- Why were the soldiers cross with the children?
- What creature did you see on page 2 and page 10?
- How did Chip know who the thief was?
- Why did Nadim brush his knees?
- What did the children bring back from this adventure?
- Why was it a good thing that the key was shiny?

OXFORD
UNIVERSITY PRESS

Great Clarendon Street, Oxford OX2 6DP

Oxford University Press is a department of the University of Oxford.
It furthers the University's objective of excellence in research, scholarship,
and education by publishing worldwide in

Oxford New York

Athens Auckland Bangkok Bogotá Buenos Aires Calcutta Cape Town
Chennai Dar es Salaam Delhi Florence Hong Kong Istanbul Karachi
Kuala Lumpur Madrid Melbourne Mexico City Mumbai Nairobi
Paris São Paulo Shanghai Singapore Taipei Tokyo Toronto Warsaw

with associated companies in Berlin Ibadan

Oxford is a registered trade mark of Oxford University Press
in the UK and in certain other countries

British Library Cataloguing in Publication Data

Data available

ISBN 0 19 919428 9

Printed in Hong Kong